Nightdances

Nightdances

James Skofield

Pictures by
Karen Gundersheimer

Harper & Row, Publishers

Nightdances
Text copyright © 1981 by James Skofield
Illustrations copyright © 1981 by Karen Gundersheimer
All rights reserved. No part of this book may be
used or reproduced in any manner whatsoever without
written permission except in the case of brief quotations
embodied in critical articles and reviews. Printed in
the United States of America. For information address
Harper & Row, Publishers, Inc., 10 East 53rd Street,
New York, N.Y. 10022. Published simultaneously in
Canada by Fitzhenry & Whiteside Limited, Toronto.
First Edition

Library of Congress Cataloging in Publication Data
Skofield, James.
    Nightdances.

    Summary: A little boy dances with his parents in the
autumn night, then back inside to bed.
    [1. Dancing—Fiction.   2. Night—Fiction.   3. Autumn
—Fiction.   4. Stories in rhyme]   I. Gundersheimer,
Karen.   II. Title.
PZ8.3.S627Ni 1981   [E]   80-8943
ISBN 0-06-025741-5   AACR2
ISBN 0-06-025742-3 (lib. bdg.)

For my mother and father   *J.S.*

For Josh, with love—remembering nighttime   *K.G.*

The sky is dark.
The house is still.
The night is dancing on the hill.

On the hill
The tall grass bends,
Singing to the autumn winds.

The autumn winds
Roar through the trees
And dance away the dying leaves.

Your windowpane
Groans and creaks.
Windmusic wakes you from warm sleep.

Rub the sleep
Out of your eyes.
Put on your robe. Tiptoe outside.

Slip past the window.

Open the door.

Moonlight is dancing on the floor.

Moonlit shiver,
Silver song.
Winds waltz silver clouds along.

Purple shadows,

Silent clouds,

Hide-and-seek dance on the ground.

Moondance, stardance,

Nightdance free.

Watch the wind dance with the trees.

Dance your own dance
With the night.
Slide in shadows. Leap in light.

Jump and tumble.
Cartwheel, weave.
Hop on the hillside. Roll in leaves.

Wind is singing.
You sing too.
Sing to the night, "Hooray! Haroooo!"

Click! The front door
Opens wide.
Mama, Papa dance outside.

Mama dancing
Swift and sweet,
Nightgown dancing 'round her feet.

Papa dancing
Strong and big,
Dancing a pajama jig.

Mama soaring
Through the air,
Playing monster with her hair.

Papa swinging
By his knees,
Playing monkey in the trees.

Dance together.
Dance alone.
Dance nightdances on the lawn—

Until the dance
Grows warm and tired.
Then slow dance, soft dance on inside.

Dance through hallways.

Dance upstairs.

Take off robe and whisper prayers.

Mama, Papa
Hug you tight.
Sweet-dream dances and good night.

Now close your eyes
And stretch your feet.
The wind will sing you back to sleep.

The sky is dark.
The house is still.
And dreams are dancing on the hill.